Head, Shoulders, Knees, and Toes

Illustrated by Jeannie Winston

ALADDIN PAPERBACKS
New York London Toronto Sydney Singapore

First Aladdin Paperbacks edition July 2003
Illustrations copyright © 2003 by Jeannie Winston

ALADDIN PAPERBACKS
An imprint of Simon & Schuster Children's Publishing Division
1230 Avenue of the Americas
New York, NY 10020

Book design by Debra Sfetsios
The text of this book was set in Century Oldstyle.

Printed in the United States of America
2 4 6 8 10 9 7 5 3 1

Library of Congress Cataloging-in-Publication Data

Winston, Jeannie.
Head, shoulders, knees, and toes / illustrated by Jeannie Winston.—
1st Aladdin Paperbacks ed.
p. cm. — (Ready-to-read)
Summary: Children and animals act out the words to a familiar song that
teaches about body parts.
ISBN 0-689-85813-2 (pbk.) — ISBN 0-689-85814-0 (hc : library edition)

1. Body, Human—Juvenile literature. [1. Body, Human.] I. Title. II.
Series.

QM27 .W555 2003
611—dc21
2002014946

Head,

shoulders,

knees,

and toes,

knees

and toes.

Head,

shoulders,

knees,

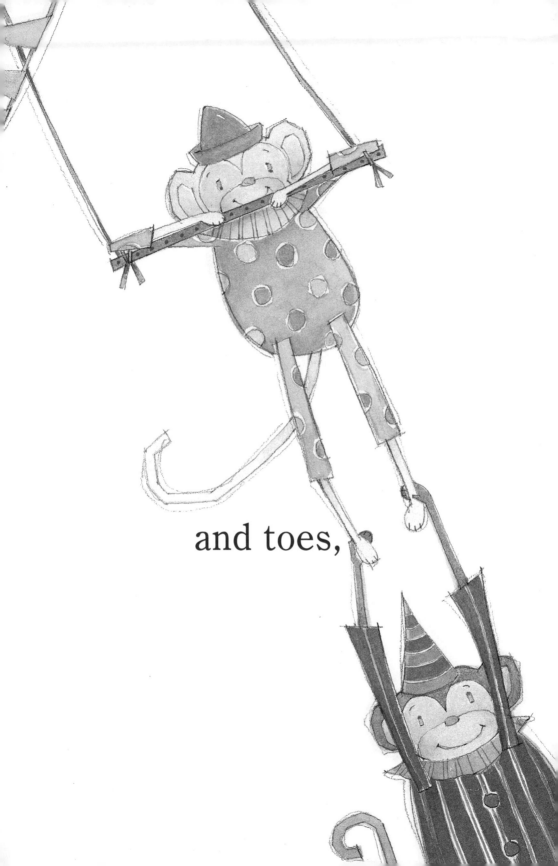

and toes,

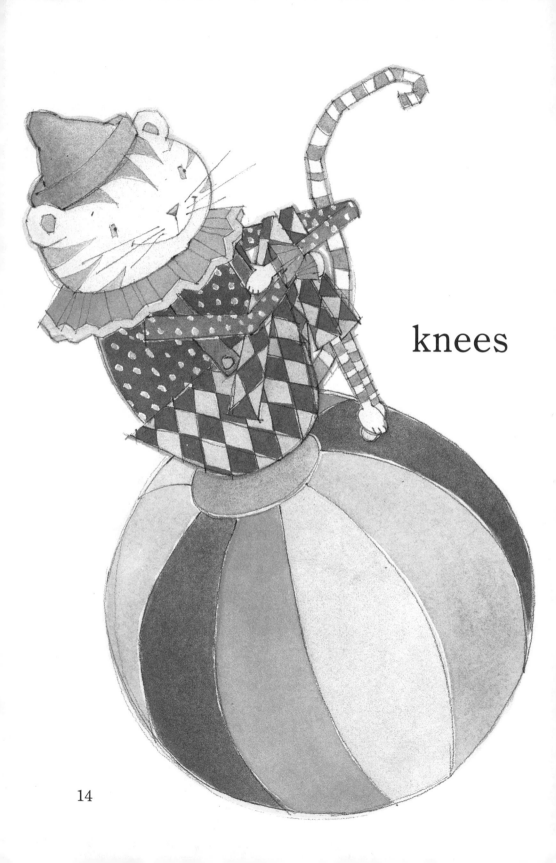

knees

14

and toes.

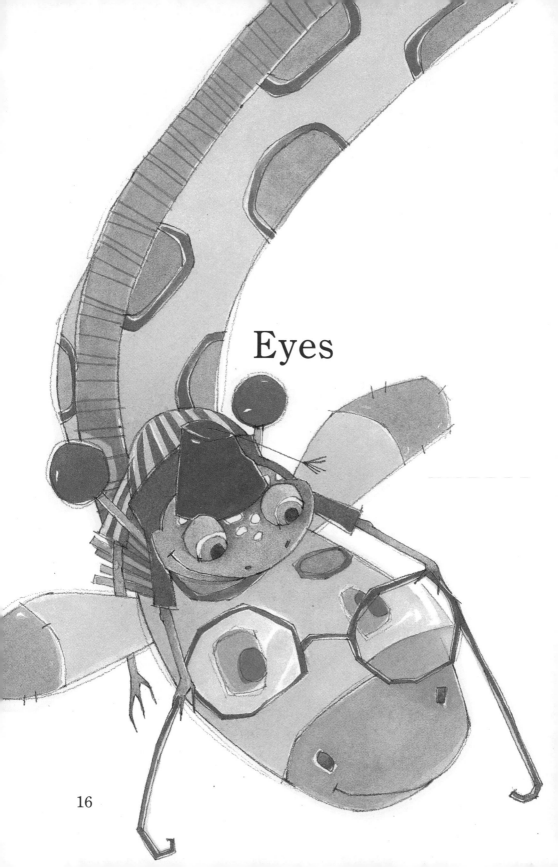

Eyes

and ears

and mouth

and nose.

Head,

shoulders,

knees,

and toes,

knees
and toes!